# Hello, Albert!

**Aimee Aryal**

Illustrated by Maura McArdle Pflueger

MASCOT BOOKS™
www.mascotbooks.com

It was a beautiful fall day at the
University of Florida.

Albert was on his way to
Ben Hill Griffin Stadium
to watch a football game.

He walked to Turlington Plaza
to meet some friends.

Some students studying near
Turlington Rock waved, "Hello, Albert!"

Albert walked across the
Plaza of Americas and stopped
in front of Smathers Library.

A professor passing by said,
"Hello, Albert!"

Albert went to Lake Alice
to see the live alligators.

The gators in the lake said,
"Hello, Albert!"

Albert stopped at the O'Connell Center
where the Gators play basketball.
He ran into the basketball coach there.

Connell Center

The coach said, "See you
next basketball season, Albert!"

It was almost time for the football game.
As Albert walked to the stadium,
he passed by some alumni.

The alumni remembered Albert
from when they went to U of F.
They said, "Hello, again, Albert!"

Finally, Albert arrived at
"The Swamp."

As he ran onto the football field
with Alberta, the crowd cheered,
"Let's Go, Gators!"

Albert watched the game
from the sidelines and
cheered for the team.

The Gators scored six points!
The quarterback shouted,
"Touchdown, Albert!"

At half-time the Pride of the Sunshine
Fightin' Gator Marching Band
performed on the field.

Albert and the crowd listened to
"Orange and Blue."

The Florida Gators won
the football game!

Albert gave the football
coach a high-five.
The coach said, "Great game, Albert!"

After the football game, Albert was tired.
It had been a long day at the
University of Florida.

He walked home and climbed into bed.

"Goodnight, Albert."

For Anna and Maya, and all of
Albert's little fans. ~ AA

For Bob, Kathleen, and Auntie Pat. ~ MMP

For information please contact Mascot Books,
P.O. Box 220157, Chantilly, VA 20153-0157.

ISBN: 1-932888-12-8

Printed in the United States.

www.mascotbooks.com

# MASCOT BOOKS
### www.mascotbooks.com

## MLB

Boston Red Sox
*Hello, Wally!*
by Jerry Remy

New York Yankees
*Let's Go, Yankees!*
by Yogi Berra

New York Mets
*Hello, Mr. Met!*
by Rusty Staub

St. Louis Cardinals
*Hello, Fredbird!*
by Ozzie Smith

## NFL

Dallas Cowboys
*How 'Bout Them Cowboys!* by Aimee Aryal

## NBA

Coming Soon

## NHL

Coming Soon

## Collegiate

Auburn University
*War Eagle!* by Pat Dye
*Hello, Aubie!* by Aimee Aryal

Boston College
*Hello, Baldwin!* by Aimee Aryal

Brigham Young University
*Hello, Cosmo!*
by Pat and LaVell Edwards

Clemson University
*Hello, Tiger!* by Aimee Aryal

Duke University
*Hello, Blue Devil!* by Aimee Aryal

Florida State University
*Let's Go 'Noles!* by Aimee Aryal

Georgia Tech
*Hello, Buzz!* by Aimee Aryal

Indiana University
*Let's Go Hoosiers!* by Aimee Aryal

Louisiana State University
*Hello, Mike!* by Aimee Aryal

Michigan State University
*Hello, Sparty!* by Aimee Aryal

Mississippi State University
*Hello, Bully!* by Aimee Aryal

North Carolina State University
*Hello, Mr. Wuf!* by Aimee Aryal

Penn State University
*Hello, Nittany Lion!* by Aimee Aryal

Purdue University
*Hello, Purdue Pete!* by Aimee Aryal

Rutgers University
*Hello, Scarlet Knight!*
by Aimee Aryal

Syracuse University
*Hello, Otto!* by Aimee Aryal

Texas A&M
*Howdy, Reveille!* by Aimee Aryal

UCLA
*Hello, Joe Bruin!* by Aimee Aryal

University of Alabama
*Roll Tide!* by Kenny Stabler
*Hello, Big Al!* by Aimee Aryal

University of Arkansas
*Hello, Big Red!* by Aimee Aryal

University of Connecticut
*Hello, Jonathan!* by Aimee Aryal

University of Florida
*Hello, Albert!* by Aimee Aryal

University of Georgia
*How 'Bout Them Dawgs!*
by Vince Dooley
*Hello, Hairy Dawg!* by Aimee Aryal

University of Illinois
*Let's Go, Illini!* by Aimee Aryal

University of Iowa
*Hello, Herky!* by Aimee Aryal

University of Kansas
*Hello, Big Jay!* by Aimee Aryal

University of Kentucky
*Hello, Wildcat!* by Aimee Aryal

University of Maryland
*Hello, Testudo!* by Aimee Aryal

University of Michigan
*Let's Go, Blue!* by Aimee Aryal

University of Minnesota
*Hello, Goldy!* by Aimee Aryal

University of Mississippi
*Hello, Colonel Rebel!*
by Aimee Aryal

University of Nebraska
*Hello, Herbie Husker!* by Aimee Aryal

University of North Carolina
*Hello, Rameses!* by Aimee Aryal

University of Notre Dame
*Let's Go Irish!* by Aimee Aryal

University of Oklahoma
*Let's Go Sooners!* by Aimee Aryal

University of South Carolina
*Hello, Cocky!* by Aimee Aryal

University of Southern California
*Hello, Tommy Trojan!*
by Aimee Aryal

University of Tennessee
*Hello, Smokey!* by Aimee Aryal

University of Texas
*Hello, Hook 'Em!* by Aimee Aryal

University of Virginia
*Hello, CavMan!* by Aimee Aryal

University of Wisconsin
*Hello, Bucky!* by Aimee Aryal

Virginia Tech
*Yea, It's Hokie Game Day!*
by Cheryl and Frank Beamer
*Hello, Hokie Bird!* by Aimee Aryal

Wake Forest University
*Hello, Demon Deacon!*
by Aimee Aryal

West Virginia University
*Hello, Mountaineer!* by Aimee Aryal

## Road Races

Marine Corps Marathon
*Run, Miles, Run!* by Aimee Aryal

Crim Festival of Races
*Running Bear and the Crim Kids!*
by Su Nottingham

Visit us online at www.mascotbooks.com for a complete list of titles.